The Monster on the Train

Written by Becca Heddle

Illustrated by Omar Aranda

Collins

We are waiting for a train in the gloom.
I scoop up my trailing scarf.

Scanning the tracks, I spot a flash of bright green near the platform.

The train appears. A bright green
monster creeps on to the train.

The green monster frowns and growls.
It slinks along the train.
I trail along too.

The monster grabs some burnt toast.
It sinks its pointed teeth into it.

The monster drops the toast crusts.
I clear them up with a broom.

It drains three cans of brown drink.
The drink spurts and stains my coat.

The monster scrubs my coat with my scarf. The stain disappears.

The monster grins. It grabs a flower for me, then starts to flee.

Thank you!

It clambers up the steep ladder to the train roof.

It runs along the train.

The monster jumps into the trees.
Its fur floats in the wind.

Is the monster asleep now, by the train tracks? Sleep tight, monster.

Monster on the tracks

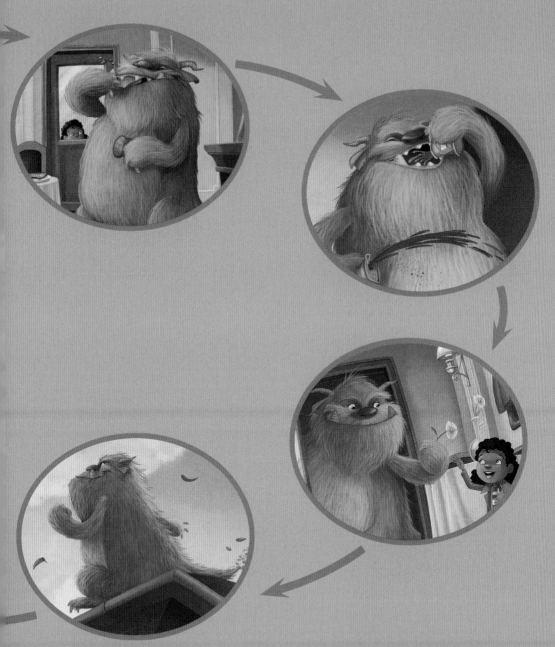

After reading

Letters and Sounds: Phase 4

Word count: 170

Focus on adjacent consonants with long vowel phonemes, e.g. /t/ /r/ /ai/ /n/

Common exception words: are, I, into, is, me, my, of, on, to, some, the, we, you

Curriculum links: History

National Curriculum learning objectives: Reading/word reading: read other words of more than one syllable that contain taught GPCs; Reading/comprehension: understand ... books they can already read accurately and fluently ... by drawing on what they already know or on background information and vocabulary provided by the teacher ... making inferences on the basis of what is being said and done

Developing fluency

- Your child may enjoy hearing you read the book.
- You could take turns to each read a page.

Phonic practice

- Model reading words with adjacent consonants and long vowel sounds. Take the word, **brown**. Say each of the sounds quickly and clearly, b/r/ow/n. Then blend the sounds together. Ask your child to do the same.
- Now ask your child to sound out and blend the following words:

  pointed   monster   bright   screech

Extending vocabulary

- The monster moves in lots of interesting ways e.g. **clambers**.
- Flick through the book and ask your child to find some interesting words that tell us the monster's movements. (*slinks, sinks, grabs, drains, creeps*)
- Can your child act out any of these words?
- Can they think of any other interesting ways the monster could move?